My Trip to the Rockies

Monika Davies

Consultants

Ryanne Kleingarn, M.A.Ed.
Social Studies Content Coordinator

Colorado Teacher Consultants

Jennifer Carpenter, M.A.Ed.
Carrie Clough, M.A.
Kristie Patrick

Publishing Credits

Rachelle Cracchiolo, M.S.Ed., *Publisher*
Aubrie Nielsen, M.S.Ed., *EVP of Content Development*
Emily R. Smith, M.A.Ed., *VP of Content Development*
Véronique Bos, *Creative Director*
Robin Erickson, *Art Director*
Dona Herweck Rice, *Senior Content Manager*
Dani Neiley, *Associate Content Specialist*

Image Credits: All images iStock and/or Shutterstock

Library of Congress Cataloging-in-Publication Data
Names: Davies, Monika, author.
Title: My trip to the Rockies / Monika Davies.
Description: Huntington Beach, CA : Teacher Created Materials, [2021] |
   "Build fluency through reader's theater"--Cover. | Audience: Grades 4-6.
   | Summary: "A fourth grade student in Colorado learns about her state
   and then goes camping in the Rockies with her family. During the trip,
   she learns about the Continental Divide, tourism in the National Park,
   Pikes Peak, and civics"-- Provided by publisher.
Identifiers: LCCN 2020047421 (print) | LCCN 2020047422 (ebook) | ISBN
   9781087630342 (paperback) | ISBN 9781087630366 (ebook)
Subjects: LCSH: Camping--Juvenile drama. | Families--Juvenile drama. |
   Rocky Mountain National Park (Colo.)--Juvenile drama. | Children's
   plays, Canadian. | Readers' theater.
Classification: LCC PR9199.4.D3844 M92 2021 (print) | LCC PR9199.4.D3844
   (ebook) | DDC 812/.6--dc23
LC record available at https://lccn.loc.gov/2020047421
LC ebook record available at https://lccn.loc.gov/2020047422

5482 Argosy Avenue
Huntington Beach, CA 92649-1039
www.tcmpub.com
ISBN 978-1-0876-3034-2

My Trip to the Rockies

Characters

May

Lee

Angela

Celeste

Ma

Mateo

Summary

The Ng family moved to Colorado during the last school year. Now it is summer, and they want to explore their state. They have decided to begin with Rocky Mountain National Park. Join them as they camp, sing, and adventure their way through their new home state.

Act 1

Setting: The Ng family driveway in Denver

Ma: All right, we made it to June first. Our first school year in Colorado is done. My three favorite kids are packed into one van. Looks like we're almost ready for our first camping trip. Now, where's Celeste?

Celeste: Present and squished in the back.

Ma: How's our food supply?

Celeste: Don't worry, Ma, I carefully followed your checklist. There are matches for the campfire. We've got pots, pans, and **utensils** packed. Breakfasts, dinners, and snacks are all covered. There's more than enough for three days of camping in Rocky Mountain National Park.

Ma: Sounds like our stomachs will stay happy on this trip. All right, how about May?

May: May reporting for duty!

Ma: Do we have everything on your campsite checklist?

4

May: Absolutely! I took my role super seriously. I wanted us completely ready to build our campsite. Our rented tent is folded up in the back. We have sleeping bags for everyone, and I made sure we have those awesome sleeping pads too. The pads are like these soft floor cushions. My friend Aimee says they'll help us sleep soundly—just like baby bears.

Lee: Wait, did you say *bears*? No one said there'd be hungry bears camping with us.

Celeste: Don't worry, black bears probably won't drop by our campsite.

May: We might see some bighorn sheep when we go hiking though.

Celeste: Or some elk. I read that during the summer, over 3,000 of them roam around the park.

Ma: Little Lee, you were in charge of entertainment. How'd that go?

Lee: Well, I knew I had the most important job, so I thought long and hard about what games to bring. I looked up a bunch of ideas online and even chatted with Celeste and May about what they'd like to play.

Celeste: We brainstormed for over two hours last week.

Ma: That's a lot of effort put into your decision, Lee! I'm **impressed**—what games did you end up bringing?

Lee: I brought one pack of cards for us to play with! Brilliant, right?

Ma: Um—okay, well… you know what, that works.

May: Sounds like we have everything—plus a pack of cards. Can we start our engines now, Ma?

Ma: Good plan—time to get this family adventure on the road!

Act 2

Setting: Glacier Basin campsite

Lee: This is a footprint?

Celeste: Well, it's a tarp from the hardware store… but yeah, it's a "footprint" for our tent.

May: We put it down on the ground, and it protects our tent from getting holes from little twigs and rocks.

Ma: Okay, let's put the footprint down here, and that'll mark our sleeping zone. Celeste and Lee, you two can lay the tent on top of it.

May: We will have a campfire, right?

Ma: Looks like there is probably a fire ring over there. We'll use it for our own fire pit.

Celeste: I'm thinking our kitchen zone should be over there. Pretty sure we should cook our food about 200 feet* from where we're sleeping so the bears stay away.

Lee: Guys, some people are coming over here—do we know them?

*60 meters

May: Hmm, I think they're park rangers.

Mateo: Hey there, campers! First time at our campground?

Ma: Is it that obvious?

Angela: Nah, you guys look like highly skilled campers. We're just checking in to see if you have been to Rocky Mountain National Park before.

Lee: Nope, it's our first time here. First time being in the Rocky Mountains, first time camping, first time hiking, first time setting up a tent, first time—

Ma: Yes, we're pretty new to all this.

Mateo: That's awesome—we love meeting first-time campers. Everything is an adventure for you all.

Angela: We're your local interpretive park rangers, by the way. I'm Angela, and my partner here is Mateo.

Lee: Local inter-what?

Mateo: Yeah, it's a long job title. We're like guardians of the park. Angela and I explain why this park is special and how you can take care of it.

Angela: We're also happy to share some ideas on what to do while you're camping here. The park is busy at the moment, but there's lots of space for everyone to have a great time.

May: Around 4.5 million visitors come to Rocky Mountain National Park every year, right?

Mateo: Spot on—you've been doing your homework on the park, huh?

Ma: She's the one who **convinced** me we should see more of Colorado.

May: Yeah, I want us to drive on Trail Ridge Road and cross the Continental Divide tomorrow!

Celeste: May has done so much **research** on this park. I almost feel like she could tell you every stick and stone we'll come across.

Ma: I thought we were going to start with some short hikes tomorrow.

Angela: There are lots of trails near the campground. Bear Lake is a quick drive away, and a few nice hikes start there. We're happy to **recommend** a couple.

Mateo: But I will say—the drive along Trail Ridge Road is incredible. I drive it every year, and it still knocks my socks off.

Angela: Around here, we call that stretch of road the "highway to the sky."

Ma: Well, it may be time for a vote.

Celeste: Our family is into **democracy**, so everyone gets a say on what group activities we do together.

Angela: That seems a fair way to decide your **itinerary**.

Ma: All those in favor of starting with some hikes near the campground tomorrow? No? Looks like it's just me. All those in favor of driving on Trail Ridge Road?

Lee: Me!

May: Me too!

Celeste: Ditto.

Ma: Seems like we have our answer.

Mateo: Let's get you all a road map!

Act 3

Setting: Trail Ridge Road

Lee: Wow.

Ma: Oh my!

Celeste: I guess the Rocky Mountains aren't just some tall hills, huh?

May: This is so much cooler than the pictures in my textbook!

Ma: It almost feels like we can touch all those clouds up here. Let's pull over and check out the view.

Lee: You guys, that sign says we're 10,759 feet* above sea level!

Celeste: Yeah, this is Milner Pass. That must be Poudre Lake over there, right?

Ma: That lake water is so clear you can see the clouds reflected in it. It's incredible what we've seen driving along this roadway.

May: You guys, did you realize we're looking right at the Continental Divide?!

*3,279 meters

Lee: You talk about this "divide" thing all the time, and I still don't know what it is.

May: Lee, you see this mountain pass we're looking at? Water that falls on that side of the pass **drains** into the Pacific Ocean. But water that falls on this side flows toward the Gulf of Mexico and the Atlantic Ocean.

Celeste: So, if rain or snow falls on this side of the mountains, it's headed east. If rain falls on the other side, it flows to the west.

Ma: You three are such smart cookies.

May: Should we hit the road now? We're not far from Grand Lake.

Lee: Is that the town where we're stopping for lunch?

Ma: Most likely—I've heard it has some nice restaurants.

Celeste: Before we get to Grand Lake, can we check out Kawuneeche (cow-uh-NEE-chee) Valley? Supposedly that's a good place to spot moose.

Lee: As long as there aren't any bears **strolling** around that valley. I'm okay with moose, but bears are a different story.

Ma: All right kids, let's get back to the car and hit the road.

May: Wait—we should take a selfie before we go! It's not every day we can get a group shot with the Rocky Mountains.

Ma: That's a great point, May—we need to document our adventure! Why don't you use my phone to take the photo?

May: Okay, big smiles everyone—and say *cheese*!

Act 4

Setting: Bear Lake

Celeste: It's only *called* Bear Lake, Lee. We've been hiking for a while now, and we haven't seen a single bear hair.

Lee: Why is this lake named after a bear then?!

Ma: Don't worry, we all know what to do if we come across a bear.

May: Throw Lee at it?

Ma: Don't tease your brother—it makes complete sense for Lee to feel nervous about seeing a bear.

Celeste: Look, there's Mateo the park ranger over there. Why don't we ask him about Bear Lake? He can probably tell us our odds of meeting up with a bear.

Mateo: Hey, it's good to see you again! How was your first night at the campground? Did you all get a good night's sleep?

May: I slept like a heavy piece of sedimentary shale.

Mateo: The shale is some of the oldest rock in the park here. You've certainly done your research, May! How about the rest of you? Enjoy your first night in the Rockies?

Celeste: It's amazing to look up and see a blanket of stars. There's hardly any light pollution out here compared to the city.

Mateo: Yes, the best part of camping for me is getting out of the city. It's peaceful in the woods, and sometimes we need a bit of silence.

Ma: Mateo, I'm hoping you can help us out with some suggestions. My son, Lee, here is worried we're—

Lee: Are there bears around here waiting to eat us?! That's all we want to know.

Mateo: Well, only black bears hang out in Rocky Mountain National Park. They aren't fans of humans, so you probably won't see one.

Lee: But what if one smells my delicious scent and decides I'm going to be its next meal?

Mateo: If you do see a bear, the best thing to do is stay calm and make lots and lots of noise. In fact, why don't we sing a song so that if there's any wildlife around, they'll know we're here. Do you have any favorite campfire songs, Lee?

Lee: How about the song we sang last night? May thought I wouldn't like it, but I actually found the song kind of funny.

Mateo: Let's hear it then!

Song: The Other Day I Met a Bear

Act 5

Setting: Glacier Basin campsite

May: I can't believe it's our last night here in the Rockies. Time has kind of whooshed by.

Celeste: Yeah, it feels good to fill up my lungs again and again with fresh mountain air.

Lee: No bears ate us for lunch either.

Ma: Don't forget, we're still going to drive up Pikes Peak tomorrow. It will be a long drive to get there! Our family trip isn't over quite yet.

May: I'm looking forward to the campfire chat that's about to start! I think Angela, the ranger, is talking about outdoor **ethics**.

Angela: Can everyone hear me?

ALL: Yes!

Angela: Excellent—hello everyone! I'm Angela, and this is Mateo. We've been park rangers at Rocky Mountain National Park for over four years now. Tonight, we're going to discuss how we can take care of the park. Let's start off with some wise words from the poet Christina Rossetti.

Poem: Hurt No Living Thing

Angela: We're all living things. And every human here is a visitor to the park. You've probably now seen some of the wild wonders of the Rocky Mountain National Park. You might've strolled through a spruce-fir forest. Maybe an elk nodded its head at you. Perhaps you took photos of Sprague Lake. Your experience of the park is your own. But, as visitors, we all have a duty to the park. We have to take care of the nature around us—and hurt no living thing.

Mateo: Has anyone heard of the Rocky **Pledge**?

Celeste: I have it written in my journal.

Mateo: How about you read it aloud to the group, Celeste?

Celeste: "To **preserve** unimpaired for this and future generations the beauty, history, and wildness therein, I pledge to protect Rocky Mountain National Park."

Angela: The Rocky Pledge is about respect. If we head into nature with respect, we step with awareness. Hopefully that means all campers consider the **impact** of their actions while in nature.

May: Is the pledge kind of like Leave No Trace ethics?

Angela: Absolutely. Leave No Trace is all about minimizing our impact on nature. It's learning to plan ahead and prepare.

Mateo: It also includes travelling and camping on **durable** surfaces and **disposing** of waste properly.

Lee: We also have to leave what we find, right?

Mateo: Exactly—any other ways we can "leave no trace"?

Celeste: We can minimize campfire impacts, respect wildlife, and be considerate of other visitors.

Angela: It's a lot to keep in mind, huh? But each principle helps us take better care of nature. That's how we protect this park for years to come.

Act 6

Setting: Glacier Basin campsite

Lee: Does this really have to be our last day of the trip? Can't we just stay on the road and keep exploring?

Ma: It's been a wonderful trip around our new home state, huh?

Lee: I don't want our Colorado adventure to end yet.

May: Me neither. It feels like we just started our adventure, and now we have to go home.

Ma: What sad faces—come on, let's enjoy the view! It's not every day we get to stand at the top of Pikes Peak.

Lee: We *are* very high up.

Celeste: Look, we can nearly see the skyscrapers in Denver!

May: Pretty sure those mountains mark the Continental Divide.

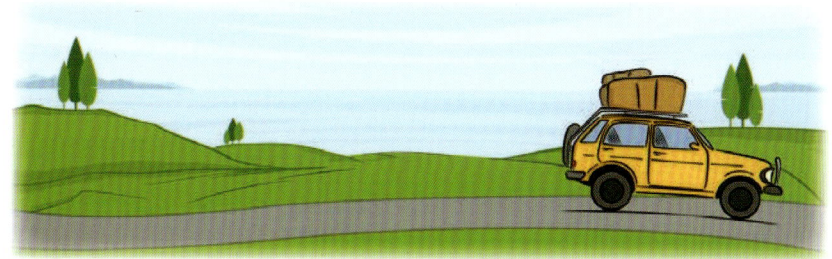

Ma: Come here, kids—it's time for a group hug. I'm so proud of us. We survived our very first camping trip, and we barely broke a sweat!

Celeste: I never doubted us for a second.

Lee: I did. Especially when we came close to being a bear snack.

May: But we made it through, and now we can say we know so much more about our new home state.

Celeste: Yeah, I feel pretty proud to call Colorado home, especially now that I know more about it.

Lee: I had a *bear*-y good time too.

May: That's a terrible joke—but agreed.

Ma: What a year it's been—and who knows what adventures we'll go on next?

Hurt No Living Thing

by Christina G. Rossetti

Hurt no living thing:
Ladybird, nor butterfly,
Nor moth with dusty wing,
Nor cricket chirping cheerily,
Nor grasshopper so light of leap,
Nor dancing gnat, nor beetle fat,
Nor harmless worms that creep.

The Other Day I Met a Bear

Traditional

The other day I met a bear,
Up in the woods, a way up there.
He looked at me, I looked at him,
He sized up me, I sized up him.
And so I ran away from there,
But right behind me was that bear.
In front of me there was a tree,
A great big tree, oh glory be!
The lowest branch was ten feet up.
I had to jump and trust my luck.
And so I jumped into the air,
But I missed that branch, a way up there.
Now don't you fret and don't you frown,
I caught that branch on the way back down.
That is the end, there ain't no more,
Unless I meet that bear once more.

Glossary

convinced—caused someone to believe that something is true

democracy—an organization or practice in which everyone is treated equally and has equal rights

disposing—throwing something away

drains—flows into, away from, or out of something

durable—staying strong and in good condition over a long period of time

ethics—rules of behavior based on ideas about what is good and bad or right and wrong

impact—a powerful or major influence or effect

impressed—filled with admiration

itinerary—the places you go to or plan to go to on a journey

pledge—a serious promise or agreement

preserve—to keep something safe from harm or loss

recommend—to say that someone or something is good and deserves to be chosen

research—the activity of getting information about a subject

strolling—walking slowly in a pleasant and relaxed way

utensils—simple tools that are used for household tasks and especially making and eating food, such as spoons